JOIN THE REBELLION!

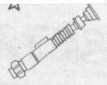

STAR WARS™

DISCOVER · WHAT · IT · TAKES

JOIN THE REBELLION!

written by **Shari Last**

CONTENTS

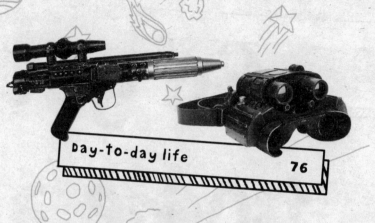

FREEDOM!

So you to be a Rebel?

want

Down with
the Empire!

Have you heard?

There's a  going on.

Conflict is building across **the galaxy,**

from the Core

to the Outer Rim.

Planets are torn apart by **civil war.** Armies of **STORMTROOPERS** terrorize big cities and small villages.

One question is on everyone's lips …

What is happening?!

Good question! Basically, a small group of good guys have decided to take on a big group of bad guys. Really bad guys.

The good guys are **FED UP** with how things are run in the galaxy, which is under the control of an **evil leader** and his loyal stormtrooper army.

There is less freedom. Innocent lives are in **danger.**
So instead of just standing around muttering, the **good guys**
have decided to REBEL—and stand up for **what's right.**

Let's call them **rebels,** OK? They've even formed
an official rebellion, with an official name:

THE ALLIANCE TO RESTORE THE REPUBLIC.

NAMING BRAINSTORM

The Alliance to Restore Freedom to the
Galaxy and Return it to a Republic

The Galactic Alliance in favor of Freedom
and Against Evil Tyrants

The We Hate Emperor Palpatine Alliance

The Mothma/Organa Effort to Find Some
Rebels And Destroy the Empire Alliance

OK,
any more
suggestions?

(This is its symbol)

We know the name isn't exactly catchy, but, for short, they are known as the **Rebel Alliance.** And if you don't have time for that either, you can just call them *rebels.*

Anyway, they are BRAVE. And **BOLD.** But there are LOTS more bad guys than good guys right now. They need as many new rebel recruits as they can get. Are you interested?

WE WANT YOU

Wait ... what will I be rebelling against?

How about the most evil, cold-hearted, power-hungry organization the galaxy has ever known?

The **GALACTIC EMPIRE.**

Boooo!

(That is its symbol)

Led by the **NASTIEST**, most **twisted** guy of all,

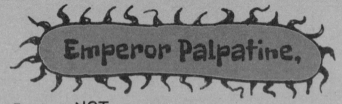

Emperor Palpatine,

the Empire is **NOT** going to make your life better.

Ah, the good old days ...

Palpatine used to be a trusted **senator** back in the days when the galaxy was a *Republic* and planets were free to rule themselves.

Look at me—I seem like a nice guy, right ... ?

Now he is in control and he will do all sorts of nasty things to keep it that way. He wants to control **every planet.** He wants to control **every resource.** He wants to control **you.**

We can have **peace** in the galaxy ...

... as long as everyone does **exactly as I say!**

Yes, you. Every single person is in danger while **the Emperor** is in charge, which is where

: THE REBELLION : comes in.

The rebels are doing everything they can to stop **the Empire.**

They **attack** Imperial bases,

destroy Imperial ships,

intercept **secret messages,**

plot, scheme, battle, outwit, and **make silly faces** at the Empire whenever they can.

But there are just **soooooo many stormtroopers!**

starfighter

big ship

really big ship

And the **Imperial Navy** is enormous!

And, worst of all, the Empire is busy scheming, and plotting, and BUILDING huge space superweapons, too.

So the Rebellion needs all the help it can get.

It needs **BRAVE**, smart recruits to join its ranks and help take down **the Empire,** one shiny, gray piece at a time.

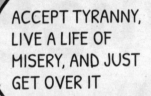

Interested? You can sign up right here by agreeing to this declaration, addressed to Emperor Palpatine himself:

To fight you and your forces by any means possible;

To refuse any Imperial law contrary to the rights of free beings;

To bring about your destruction and the destruction of the Galactic Empire;

To make forever free all beings in the galaxy.

X ....

Ready? **Let's GO!**

A rebellion **STARTS OFF** with just **one** or **two** people who look at the way things are and say a big, FAT

NO!

Ezra Bridger was a young kid who did just that. He started by collecting **stormtrooper helmets.** But then he joined a group of rebels and realized he could make the galaxy **a better place**—and maybe add even more helmets to his collection.

Now he's part of the rebel **GHOST** crew, along with Hera Syndulla (whose dad, Cham, was also a rebel), Jedi Kanan Jarrus, Sabine Wren, and Zeb Orrelios. Oh, and a **grumpy** little droid named Chopper.

That's their ship, the *Ghost*

Chopper— grumpy

Hera—pilot

Kanan—Jedi

Zeb— warrior

Sabine— artist

Ezra— rebellious

This group does what it can to defeat **the Empire** on the planet **Lothal.**

Slowly, these 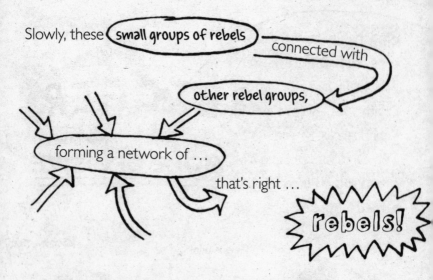 small groups of rebels connected with other rebel groups, forming a network of ... that's right ...

rebels!

Eventually, a couple of key rebel folk, including **Mon Mothma** and **Bail Organa,** decided to make it official and they launched the snappily titled **Alliance to Restore the Republic. Hooray!**

ALLIANCE TO RESTORE THE REPUBLIC LAUNCH PARTY

REBEL STUFF

It made sense to start coordinating all these rebel missions, in the hope that it would lead to

BIGGER

MORE DECISIVE

victories.

The founders of **THE ALLIANCE** are a **serious** bunch, but hey, they have a **serious job** to do. They still enjoy a good joke once in a while, though—I mean, they're not **the Empire.**

It takes a lot of **courage** to rebel against an army **MUCH LARGER** than yours. But we know it can be done—because it's been done before! During the *Clone Wars*, there was **a civil war** on the planet **Onderon.**

We didn't do it on our own-deron.

You're not funny, Saw.

Saw Gerrera and his sister, **Steela,** led a rebellion against those who had **taken control** of their homeland. Their victory showed everyone what a bunch of determined rebels can do.

YEARS LATER, Saw joined forces with the Rebel Alliance, even though they **disagreed** on many issues, to stand up to the threat of the Empire. The rebels needed all the help they could get!

Spot the difference
Years of rebelling had a heavy impact on Saw's health.

Plastoid armor

Onderonian banner worn as cape

Ventilator breathing tube

Walking stick carved from dxunwood

Cybernetic foot plate

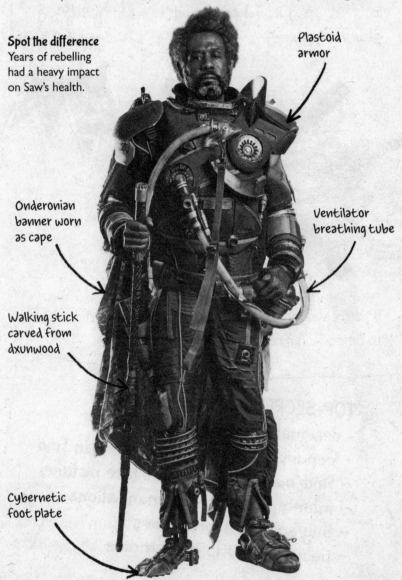

Founding a rebellion is **A PRETTY BIG JOB,** so it pays to be **organized.** (Actually, there is very little payment involved. Apart from **honor** and **glory,** of course!)

If you're wondering what **sort of things** need to be done in a rebellion, **look no further:**

TOP-SECRET REBELLION CHECKLIST:
- designate leaders
- repurpose any starships we can find
- find/build a secret base (see picture)
- intercept enemy communications
- buy some holoprojectors
- bring an end to the Empire ...

Tower—good for keeping a lookout

Thick wall—good for defense

Thick jungle—good for hiding in

And that's before you even get *started* with all the top-secret **missions** and **space battles.** But even before all of those things, a rebellion needs something FUNDAMENTAL. Something that is hard to **find,** even harder to **replace,** and absolutely **essential**—some rebels!

SO HOW DOES THE REBEL ALLIANCE RECRUIT NEW REBELS?

EASY! They look for anyone who has a reason to **HATE** the Empire. Admittedly, it's **not very hard** to find people who dislike *tyranny,* **violence**, and *stormtroopers taking over* their homeworlds, but sometimes, a rebellion needs a person with a little *EXTRA* reason.

Take **Jyn Erso,** for example. Her father was *forced* to build the Empire's deadly superweapon, the Death Star. Now there's **a good reason** to become a rebel. Granted, when the rebels found her, she was **in prison,** so it didn't look **LOOK** like she would make a good rebel ...

Possible rebel recruits:

No   Maybe

But Jyn turned out to be a **REAL HERO,** even if she wasn't very good at **listening to the rules.** Then again, isn't that the very **definition** of a rebel, anyway?

Excuse me—ooof!

BASH!

I'm not listening!

I wouldn't bother if I were you.

Definitely not.

Once you have your ~~Empire-hating~~ rebel recruits raring
to go, it's a good idea to come up with some sort of **strategy.**

Plans can be **TOP SECRET,** secret, or not secret at all.
(But as everyone knows, top secret ones are the **coolest!**)

> Psst: there's
> a plan to throw
> Admiral Ackbar a
> secret surprise party!

> I'm Admiral
> Ackbar, you fool!

Every rebel **BASE** has a **high-tech briefing room**
where the **smartest military minds** devise battle
tactics and brief the rebels about upcoming missions.

Rebel briefing room: full of secret plans, and sometimes panic.

Everyone has a chance to voice their **ideas,** unlike the **Empire,** which is a **dictatorship**—just the **Emperor** gets to decide what to do.

The plan is: we need a plan!

Good idea!

BLOW UP!

Try to keep it simple

OK, not that simple

Next, the rebel leaders find out what everyone's **STRENGTHS** are so they can put them to **good use** ...

What are **your** strengths?

A rebel's strengths and **skills** will determine the **TYPE** of job they can do for the Rebellion. There are all sorts of roles that need filling: **pilots, soldiers,** *spies,* MEDICS, **chefs, mechanics, computer programmers, administrators, personnel** (the people looking after all the people, not at the front of the action), and more.

Pilot

Soldier

Radio operator

Medic

Mechanic

Programmer

SCARED of HEIGHTS? Don't become a pilot. Can't **tell the difference** between a Death Star and a forest moon? Don't work in intelligence. And if you think roasted Kowakian monkey-lizard tastes good, **don't** be a **chef.**

Meet the REBELS

You'll be in famous company in the Rebel Alliance. Try not to get starstruck if you meet any of these well-known faces.

LEIA ORGANA

Leia is a **princess** from the planet Alderaan. She is known for her quick wits and her "cinnamon buns" hairstyle.

LUKE SKYWALKER

Luke is training to be a Jedi. His **Force skills** make him one of the best rebel pilots of all time.

ADMIRAL ACKBAR

This Mon Calamari is
Supreme Commander
of the **Alliance Fleet.**
He's a real old-timer,
with tons of experience.

LANDO CALRISSIAN

Once a conman and gambler,
Lando is now the most
charming and **stylish**
general in the Alliance.

MON MOTHMA

This classy **Chandrilan** founded
the Rebel Alliance with Leia's
adoptive dad, Bail Organa, and
birth mom, Padmé Amidala.

JYN ERSO

Tough cookie Jyn is the
daughter of a scientist forced
to work on the Empire's
Death Star superweapon.

You might have noticed that some of the rebels are **also** JEDI. But being a **Jedi** is very different to being a **rebel**.

lightsaber

blaster

Jedi

☑ fights evil
☑ uses a lightsaber
☑ uses the Force

Rebel

☑ fights evil
☑ doesn't use a lightsaber
☑ can't use the Force

These days, there are only a few Jedi left in the galaxy—thanks to Emperor Palpatine's **evil** (but unfortunately **very successful**) plan to wipe them out. For years, the Jedi have had to remain **in hiding.**

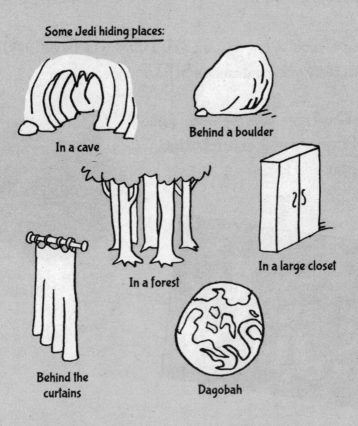

Some Jedi hiding places:

In a cave

Behind a boulder

In a forest

In a large closet

Behind the curtains

Dagobah

So it makes sense that the surviving **Jedi** would join forces with the rebels to help take down the Empire—and best of all, to **stop** Palpatine **once and for all.**

So what do the rebels actually do? Well, they **BATTLE**, of course! Some rebel battles have gone **down in history** as the most **daring, inventive,** and awesome battles of **ALL TIME.**

An early rebel victory was the **Battle of Lothal,** which really made the Empire **SIT UP** and take notice.

The *Ghost* crew gave the whole galaxy **HOPE** after they liberated **Lothal** from Imperial forces.

Ghost Crew

The Battle of Lothal took place on many fronts, but it involved **1.** *Tricking* all the stormtroopers on the planet into boarding a mobile Imperial base, before **2. LAUNCHING** that base into space, and then **3.** *Blasting* it to smithereens.

Mission complete.

Rebel warfare started **small:** Liberating **individual planets,** taking down an **Imperial officer** here, a **stormtrooper battalion** there, and destroying weapons facilities **one at a time.**

But as the rebel **strategy** grew bigger and **BIGGER,** coordinated attacks across the galaxy became possible. No rebel victory promised as much **HOPE** as the destruction of **the first Death Star.**

PICTURE THE SCENE:

BIG Death Star Superweapon that can **destroy** a whole planet with just one blast from its **SUPERLASER.**

Tiny little rebel **X-wings.**

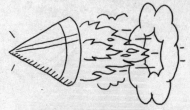

Two even tinier **proton torpedoes.**

Proton torpedo finds a **single exhaust port** on the Death Star, starts a chain reaction, and **BOOM!** Bye bye Death Star. **HELLO history books!**

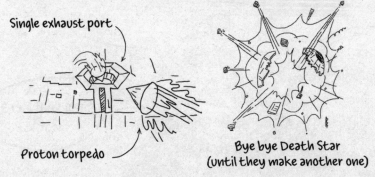

Single exhaust port

Proton torpedo

Bye bye Death Star
(until they make another one)

41

The Empire did not let that defeat stop them.
They built **AN EVEN BIGGER DEATH STAR.**

They came up with a great name for this one, too ... Death Star II

Still, the Empire never really *learns* from its **mistakes,** does it? It keeps thinking **BIGGER** is better, but the rebels know **SMALL** can be **MIGHTY,** too (just ask Yoda).

Size matters not!

So the rebels **don't lose hope** after hearing about this **new Death Star**—even though it's as **BIG** as a **MOON.**

Rebels, we must not lose hope!

There's a **super fierce battle,** both on the planet moon of **Endor** and up in **space.** After quite a few setbacks, rebel perseverance wins out and the second Death Star is **DESTROYED!**

Yub Nub!

Gwarrhh.*

*I hope I get a medal this time.

It's not all about blowing up Imperial bases. Being part of a rebellion means facing **defeat** as often as (or even **MORE** than) celebrating **victory:**

I hope I turned the stove off!

Oops! This Imperial probe droid has found the rebel base on Hoth.

Found you!

Bye!

Oops! Hoth has been evacuated.

Oops! Han has been frozen in carbonite.

Planets can be **obliterated,** bases can be *attacked,* battles can be **lost,** starships can be **gunned down,** and people you thought were allies can **betray** you (looking at you, **Lando Calrissian**).

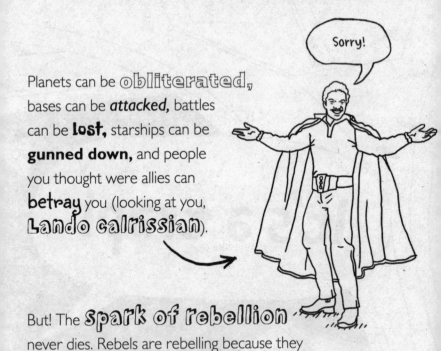

Sorry!

But! The **spark of rebellion** never dies. Rebels are rebelling because they have **hope** for a **better future.** So if you want to make it past the **bad times,** you have to get back up and carry on.

And here's a piece of **advice** to help avoid future

DISASTER:

ALWAYS be on the **LOOKOUT** for an Imperial **trap ...**

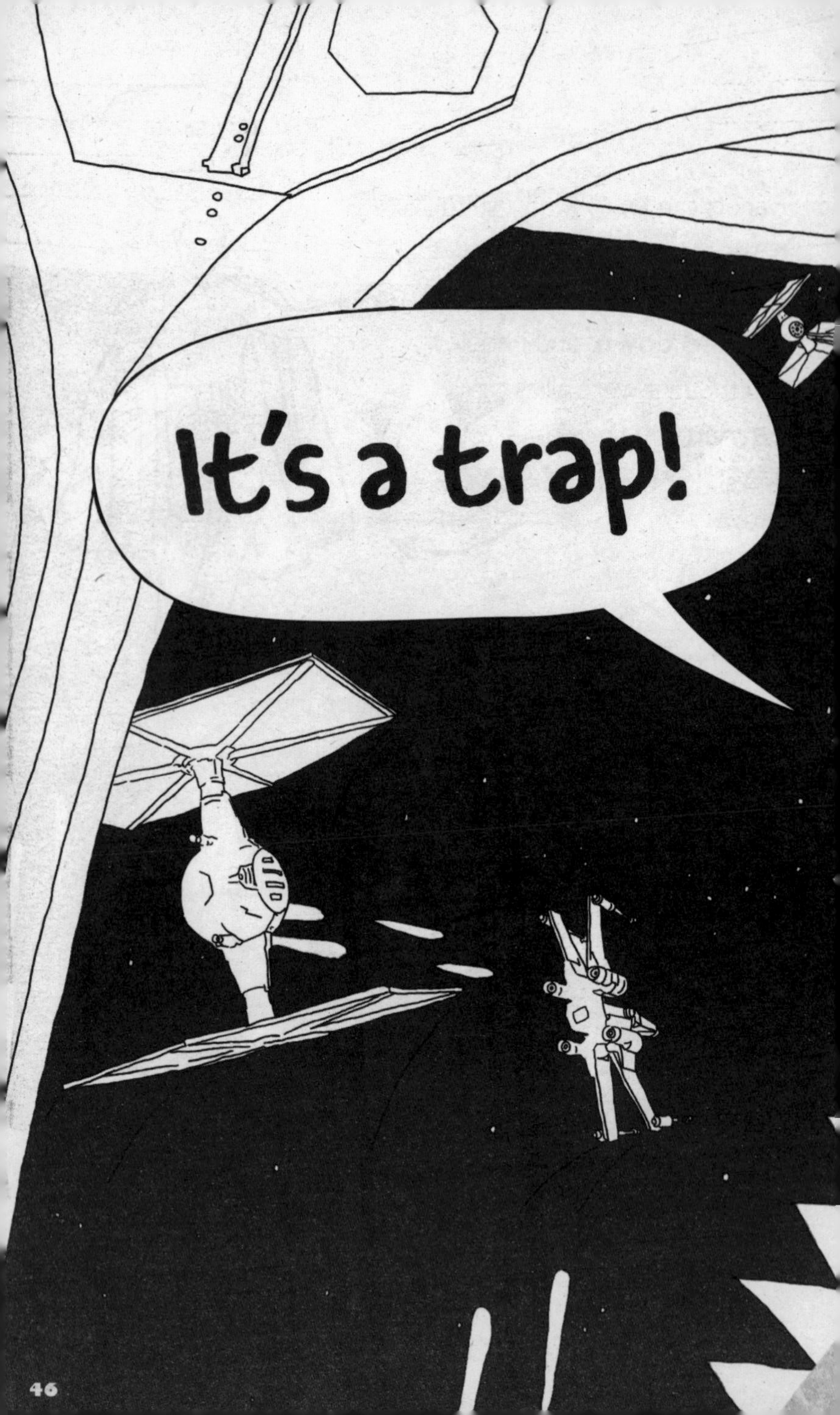
It's a trap!

When things take a turn for the **worse,**
what can you do?

You can **curl up in a ball and cry,**
but we don't recommend that.

You can 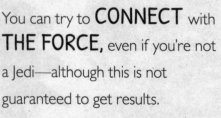 **flee.**

You can try to *fix the situation.*

You can try to **CONNECT** with
THE FORCE, even if you're not
a Jedi—although this is not
guaranteed to get results.

Of course, you could try
to **fight back.**

*Put your black belt
on and karate your
way out of there!*

Sometimes, rebels choose to face **ALMOST CERTAIN DEFEAT** to help the Rebellion **complete its mission**. Being prepared to make big **SACRIFICES** is a **KEY** part of being a rebel.

It is best to **avoid** these situations if the aim is **SURVIVAL**, but things have a way of getting **out of control, especially** where the **Empire** is concerned. Just ask the **FORCE GHOST** of Jedi Obi-Wan Kenobi:

It was my time and I needed to give the rebels a chance to escape.

Rebels are **selfless, brave, daring,** *loyal,*
often **FUNNY,** and sometimes a 𝕝𝕚𝕥𝕥𝕝𝕖 𝕓𝕚𝕥 𝕤𝕚𝕝𝕝𝕪.
And every rebel counts.

Excuse me, have you seen Chewie anywhere?

Unlike the Empire, which has **HUGE ARMIES** the
Emperor sees as **expendable,** the rebels value their soldiers.

We just lost more than 1,000 soldiers in that battle and—

You should try telling someone who cares.

Each rebel gets to make **THEIR OWN** choices and has the potential to make a **HUGE** difference. Whether that's by firing a proton torpedo into a very small hole, becoming **one with the Force*** to save their friends, or risking it all to **STEAL secret Imperial plans.**

*Jedi-speak for dying

If you strike me down, I shall come back as a Force ghost and haunt you—wooo!

SO HOW WILL *YOU* HELP THE REBELLION?

what does it take to be a REBEL?

Being a rebel is about more than just *dodging stormtroopers* and **destroying Death Stars,** although those are definitely TOP OF THE LIST of **"rebel things to do"** ...

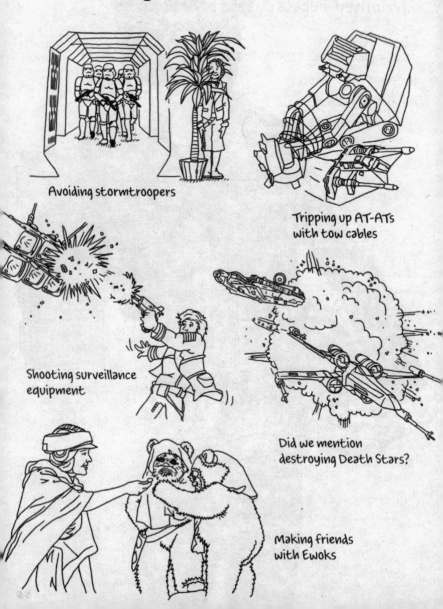

Avoiding stormtroopers

Tripping up AT-ATs with tow cables

Shooting surveillance equipment

Did we mention destroying Death Stars?

Making friends with Ewoks

Rebels need all sorts of **very specific skills,** whether for **planning** missions, actually **going on** missions, or even just helping to keep the secret base nice and tidy while **other rebels** plan and go on missions.

Training and practice will help a rebel to learn these skills.

Good, good, excellent camouflage choices.

But I can't see Cassian Andor anywhere ...

Well done Andor, you've won this week's camouflage challenge!

Above all, rebels need to be **loyal, daring, brave,** and **resourceful.**

A rebel might need to get past an **Imperial checkpoint** one day. The **best way** to do this is ...

... UNDETECTED, OF COURSE! Therefore, rebels need to be **extra sneaky.**

HOW TO SNEAK PAST STORMTROOPERS 101

1. Spot stormtroopers

2. Don't let THEM spot YOU!

Jyn Erso and her team of **ROGUE REBELS** once used a borrowed *(stolen)* Imperial cargo ship to land on the planet 𝕾𝖈𝖆𝖗𝖎𝖋. By giving the correct **clearance codes,** they were allowed through the **shield gate.**

But just because they've managed to get past **security,** doesn't mean it's time to can **relax.** The mission has **only just begun!**

And don't forget that other word we mentioned before—
courage.

Being a rebel means you are at risk ALL. THE.
TIME. Even the **sweetest old lady rebel** is at
risk from an Empire that wants to crush her. It takes
COURAGE to stand up to that.

Courage is *essential* on a mission. So many things can go wrong. Take the Battle of Scarif, for example: almost **nothing** went to plan. Rebels Jyn Erso and Cassian Andor ended up having to retrieve the Death Star plans **on their own** and transmit them manually despite all their original, high-tech plans.

Is it brave for a few rebels plus a droid to take on an entire planet of shoretroopers when the Empire has built a gigantic space weapon?

Um, actually, maybe that's foolish rather than brave—

Nah, I think it's brave. Come on!

But even in the face of defeat, **they never gave up.**

Rebellions need **secret information**. They need **spies**. Would **you** be a good undercover agent?

Rebel **Ezra** once pretended to be a cadet at an Imperial Academy in order to **STEAL A DECODER.**

Ezra UNDERCOVER

He made it out just in time, because the **Inquisitor** was coming—sent by Darth Vader to **hunt down** rebels—and he would have **recognized** Ezra's face. Note: You **CANNOT** change your face, so keep this in mind.

Alexsandr Kallus was an **unexpected** rebel spy. He was an **Imperial officer,** but, after learning more about the Rebellion, decided to use his position in the Empire to pass **SECRET INFORMATION** to the rebels. He used a code name:

"FULCRUM."

This is a code name that lots of other rebels have used across the years. Jedi **Ahsoka Tano** was the first to suggest it.

What kind of a code name is Fulcrum, anyway?

Actually, it's a pretty good code name because a "fulcrum" is a thing that plays a crucial role in an event, so ...

With the Empire **breathing down their necks** all the time, and chasing them all across the galaxy, rebels must send their communications **secretly.**

Whether you use **CODE NAMES,** passwords, **secret handshakes,** or hide your message inside a droid, it's essential to stay *one step ahead* of the enemy.

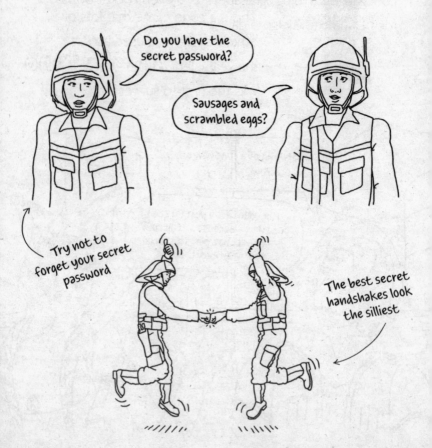

Do you have the secret password?

Sausages and scrambled eggs?

Try not to forget your secret password

The best secret handshakes look the silliest

Princess Leia

once hid a secret **call for help** inside her reliable astromech droid, **R2-D2.**

In fact, R2-D2 has lots of **secret compartments,** which come in useful for many things: secret messages, cool gadgets, hiding lightsabers, and even rocket boosters for **FLYING** away from danger! Never underestimate a droid. A rebel should always keep one around.

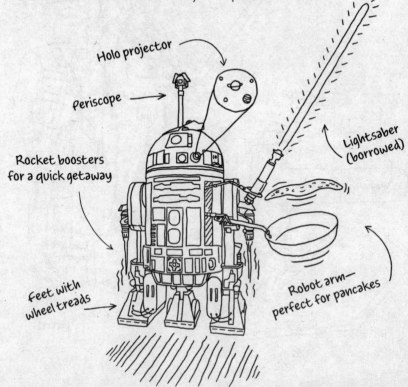

Holo projector

Periscope →

← Rocket boosters for a quick getaway

Lightsaber (borrowed)

Feet with wheel treads →

Robot arm— perfect for pancakes

Speaking of **secret compartments,** rebels often need to **smuggle forbidden items** from place to place. Things like weapons, people wanted by the Empire, and of course, *stolen Death Star plans.*

Therefore, it is useful to have a few **smuggler friends** who know all the best hyperspace routes and have plenty of **secret spaces** on their **starships** for hiding things.

Grrrr!*

Hey fuzzball, put it down!

Can I come out now?

*Grrrr!

Han Solo is one such smuggler. He is recruited by the rebels to move **R2-D2** to a rebel base **undetected.** Han's smuggler knowledge comes in **USEFUL** and he is able to help the rebels in their attack on the Death Star. He even joins the rebels (although it takes him a while to make up his mind).

MEET THE SCOUNDRELS

CHEWIE
Copilot and muscle

HAN SOLO
Smuggler and
Kessel Run champ

LANDO
Smooth talker and
master negotiator

Lots of the time, the outcome of a mission will depend on whether or not you can get past a **Stormtrooper.** A rebel's best bet is to **tricking them** because, let's be honest, they are **EASILY FOOLED.** Stormtroopers are not the most **strong-minded** of people.

Even if you aren't a Jedi and thus able to use the Force to carry out a **MIND TRICK,** like the **famous trooper-tricker, Obi-Wan Kenobi,** you can always try the **OLD SHOULDER-TAP TRICK.** Or even a basic **"Oh, look!"** might work.

IMPORTANT IMPERIAL STUFF

Fooling stormtroopers is a very useful skill for rebels.

HERE ARE SOME KEY PHRASES
TO LEARN, JUST IN CASE:

"You will let me out of my cell."

"These aren't the droids you're looking for."

"I am going to escape now and it's OK."

"You will give me the secret files."

"Bring me a chicken sandwich."

"You will do a dance for Darth Vader later."

Rebels often need to **infiltrate** an enemy base. Jyn and Cassian had to get inside the **archives** on **Scarif,** Han and Luke needed to rescue Princess Leia from the **Death Star,** and Han and Leia had to destroy the shield generator on the Forest Moon of Endor, which was **guarded** by the Empire's forces.

Sometimes a good **disguise** will do the trick. (Make sure it is a **good** disguise, however.)

What sort of disguise is that?

It's all I could find, kid.

Other times, enlisting the help of the **locals** is a good strategy. And sometimes, just running up and banging on the front door will be the **LAST THING** the enemy expects.

Just make sure you have an exit strategy—or a **Wookiee** like **Chewbacca** to bail you out when things get sticky.

Guess what? Sometimes things go **wrong.** That's right. It's not always perfect all the time in the Rebellion.

Part of rebel life is **adapting to change.** When Darth Vader finds your secret base on not-secret-enough ice planets like Hoth, there's no time for regret. You must be prepared to flee at a moment's notice.

Let's get out of here!

Grab the most important stuff, destroy the rest, distract the approaching enemy, and *make a run for it.*

Escaping doesn't mean you are not brave. If it's a losing battle, the smart thing to do is run—live to fight another day and **find another base** to hide in. Take down as many AT-ATs as you can along the way. At the **Battle of Hoth,** this is exactly what the rebels managed to do.

As we said, secret missions often mean **disguises.**
You will need to know which disguises will help you
blend in. Therefore:

A rebel may have to wear **Imperial uniforms** to infiltrate an enemy base.

Or they might have to dress as a **BOUNTY HUNTER** to go unnoticed in an underworld hangout.

Princess Leia once dressed as the bounty hunter **Boushh** to rescue Han Solo from Jabba's palace. She even **altered her voice** so Jabba wouldn't suspect. Unfortunately, removing her helmet gave the game away.

75

-DAY LIFE

For a rebel, every day is **different.** No week is the same. On a Monday they might be getting their starships ready for **BATTLE** or **uploading star charts** to their navigation droids.

Droid port

X-wing fighter

Navigation droid

On Tuesday they might be trying to **crack Imperial codes** or plant **false information trails.** Perhaps they're making sure the base's **shield generators** are working.

So, are the shield generators working?

Steve, it's Monday today— we should be uploading star charts to the droids. Generators are tomorrow.

Maybe by Wednesday they're trekking through a **wild jungle** on a top-secret rescue mission.

Sometimes it might feel like a rebel's job is **small** or **unimportant.** But remember that there are rebels **all across** the galaxy, each doing a small job, and lots of small jobs add up make a **BIG DIFFERENCE.**

The Rebel Alliance has a **fleet.** Let's not compare it to the **SHINY** Imperial Navy, OK? That will just make you **sad.**

Still, rebels are very **technological** and **creative.** They have taken old starships and updated them for their own needs.

X-WING
A classic—very fast and good for dodging enemy fire.

U-WING
For dropping soldiers close to the ground, right in the action.

Starfighters, bombers, and **assault ships** have been upgraded and are ready for **fierce rebel battles.**

B-WING
Rebels need to attack, not just run away, so having varied, capable ships is a necessary part of the fleet.

Y-WING
Some of the oldest ships in the fleet, but these bombers are sturdy and reliable.

Now all the rebels need to do is decide *which* ships to use for their missions. Do they need HYPERSPEED? **Defense** shields? Firepower? To try not to be **seen?**

on land, the rebels must borrow whatever vehicles they can find and make them work. They're *scrappy* like that. From **skimmers** to **landspeeders** and everything in between, rebels must be prepared to hop aboard anything and get it going.

Like this one time, on the Forest Moon of Endor, **LUKE AND LEIA** (and a few furry, little Ewoks) got hold of some **Imperial speeder bikes.**

Jedi reflexes are very useful in this moment.

Watch out for that branch!

Those bikes are **fast!** They were a little hard to master, but Luke and Leia are *exceptional*, and even defeated a few **scout troopers.**

Chewie actually saved the day on **Endor** by commandeering one of the Empire's **AT-ST** walkers, learning how to control it in almost no time, and using its **cannons** to fire on some very **confused** stormtroopers.

A rebel also needs to be comfortable using **a wide range** of **weapons** and **gadgets.**

From **BLASTERS** and more unusual weapons like **BOWCASTERS** or **CANONS** to explosive **THERMAL DETONATORS,** and more, a rebel needs to make the most out of whatever tools they have on hand.

I am armed and dangerous!

It's also really useful to be **well-versed in technology.** You don't want to be setting your **thermal detonator timer** wrong, or putting that **JETPACK** on upside down.

From **comlinks** to **holoprojectors,** communication is key. Receiving holograms can be tricky, however—especially when there is poor holonet signal. *(We're talking about you, sandy-planet-in-the-middle-of-nowhere Tatooine!)*

PEWW!

Rebel blaster

Comlink

Grappling hook

Thermal detonator

Don't forget your backpack or utility belt to keep all your gear in!

Quadnoculars

Quadnoculars—essential for spotting incoming danger before it's too late.

As well as **technology and gadgets,** rebels need to **rely** on other people. Joining the Rebellion means meeting lots of *like-minded* people:

People who are prepared to **stand up** to the Empire no matter what. People who want to feel like they're part of something **BIG** and **important.** People who also think retro **ARC-170s** are **super cool.**

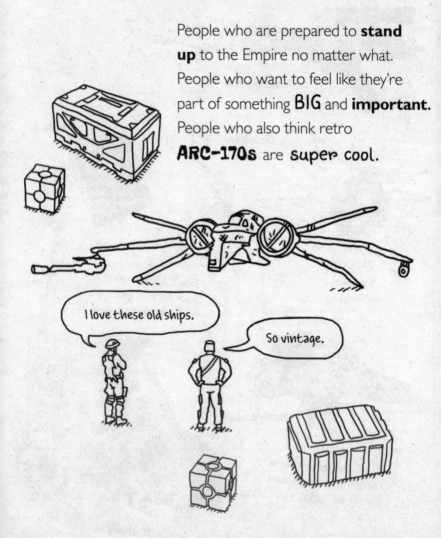

I love these old ships.

So vintage.

Many **epic friendships** have been forged between rebel colleagues, such as Ezra and Sabine, Jyn and Cassian, and Luke and Han. These pals are prepared to rescue one another from the *scariest* of **situations.**

Scary situation:
Nearly eaten by Ewoks

Scary situation: Stuck
in a trash compactor

Cover me,
I'm going in!

I don't think that's
what he meant, Zeb.

And there's nothing like knowing that a **good friend** has your **BACK** during a battle.

Did I mention **DROIDS** yet? Rebel droids are the **BEST!** Not only do they have all sorts of *amazing* uses, such as starship hacking and secret-message hiding, they also have their own **personalities.**

Unlike **boring Imperial droids,** whose memories get wiped frequently, some rebel droids are allowed to *keep* their memories, which build up **unique** personalities over time.

The rebels know that this can be quite useful—*most* of the time. It also means droids become more than objects— they become **FRIENDS** to rely on.

I've had amnesia for as long as I can remember.

For a **sarcastic beep,** look no further than *astromech droid* R2-D2, who can fix machines in space—or anywhere at all.

Beep! Dooopp!! Wooop?

If you want a droid to **WORRY** over you, kind of like a parent, then find *protocol droid* C-3PO, who was built for **communication**.

If you need help pranking your friends, call Chopper.

Or for a friendly thumbs up, hang out with BB-8.

Rebels should not just expect to make *new friends.*
They can expect to make lots of new **ENEMIES,** too.

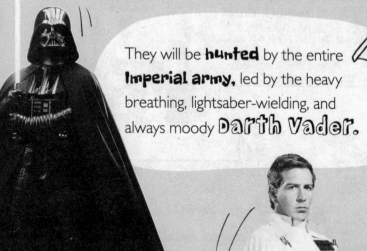

They will be **hunted** by the entire **Imperial army,** led by the heavy breathing, lightsaber-wielding, and always moody **Darth Vader.**

Determined officers—like Director **Orson Krennic**—will track them down.

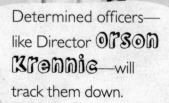

Red-eyed, ruthless villains like Grand Admiral **Thrawn** will chase them across the galaxy.

Stormtroopers, snowtroopers, sand troopers, swamp troopers, shoretroopers (you get the picture) will **patrol,** *search,* **battle,** and 𝖒𝖆𝖗𝖈𝖍 just about everywhere on the orders of the Empire.

DON'T MESS WITH SSIDIOUSsS

Darth SIDIOUS

BEWARE OF THE SITH LORD!

Oh, and there's a **scary-faced Sith Lord** controlling it all. No point in hiding—it's just about **KEEPING OUT OF REACH.**

With the Empire's soldiers out *hunting* for rebels, **no place is safe.** And 𝕊𝕖𝕔𝕣𝕖𝕥 𝕣𝕖𝕓𝕖𝕝 𝕓𝕒𝕤𝕖𝕤 never end up staying secret for long.

I'VE GOT A BAD FEELING ABOUT THIS ...

The Empire spends a lot of time trying to find rebel bases and, **as a result,** the rebels spend a lot of time **EVACUATING** one base and *finding* their next one.

Things to avoid when finding a new secret rebel base ...

... The Death Star (the Empire's own, terrible base)

Yavin 4 was the rebels' base for a short time, hidden in an old, large **temple** on a JUNGLE MOON.

Echo Base, their headquarters on **ICE PLANET HOTH,** was hidden deep within the planet's snowy confines—a perfect **(although cold)** hiding place … until it was discovered by, of course, the Empire, **wielding cannon fire.**

It's a bit like a game—except it's the most **dangerous** game you might **EVER PLAY.** Oh, and the other team are **REALLY, REALLY, REALLY** sore losers!

You always get to be the car! It's not fair!

Yes but you always roll the dice first!

So don't get **TOO COMFORTABLE** because at any moment the Empire might **track you down,** which means it's

TIME TO GO!

A wise rebel should always have their next base ready. Maybe it's on a planet like Crait, which is *hidden behind a bigger planet?*

I don't think they can see us!

Shhhhhh!

Maybe it's camouflaged by ancient **pyramid-like structures** (Yavin 4, again.)

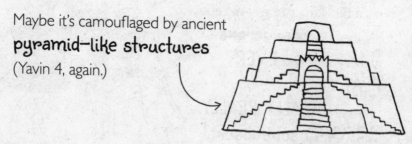

Ziggurat
(pyramid-like structure)

Maybe it's part of a **large, gnarly tree,** like **YODA'S** secret hideout on **Dagobah.**

Find me here, they will not.

But stationary bases haven't always stood the test of time … Maybe it's time to get a *mobile* base. One that can travel **with** the rebels and **away** from the Empire.

Hyperdrive generator

One of the rebels' best ideas was to set up their base on board the *Home One,* a big, Mon Calamari **star cruiser** that has the advantage of being able to **escape** from the Empire through **hyperspace.**

When you're with the rebels and **in a tight spot**—and there will be many of these, believe me—only *quick thinking* can save the day and avert certain **DISASTER.**

This fire is making any thinking a bit difficult ...

For example, if you're about to be served as the **main course** at an all-you-can-eat Ewok buffet, as Luke, Han, and Chewie were on Endor, you'd better keep your **wits** about you.

Don't mess around with
JEDI MIND TRICKS, who knows
if they will work on an **Ewok.**

Don't even bother!

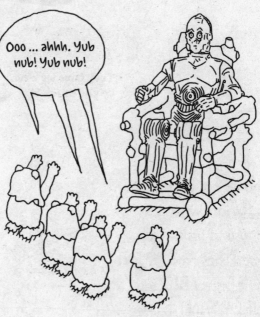

Ooo ... ahhh. Yub nub! Yub nub!

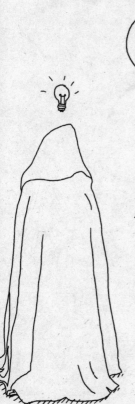

Getting your droid to **PRETEND** to be
a *holy golden god* should do
the trick, though.

Remember that.

Like all **good teams,**
rebels join together in times
of loss and defeat,
supporting one
another and *promising*
to continue their rebellion
for as long as they can.

That time we blew
up the Death Star

And it's *not always* doom
and gloom when you
choose to fight as a
rebel. They have **WON**
some pretty **BIG** and
IMPORTANT battles.

And then after those **victories,**
the rebels love to **celebrate!**

Rauwrrruwh warrgh ...!*

There's nothing quite like
a rebel celebration—we're
talking dancing, fancy foods,
fireworks, and awards
ceremonies. Come on,
who wouldn't want
a rebel medal?

*I'd like a medal ...!

YOU CAN'T THE RESIS

The Empire might have been *toppled* (hooray for the Rebel Alliance!), but there are **ALWAYS** more bad guys waiting to do bad things. And bad guys need more people to fight them.

Next up is the First Order.

This is its symbol

Guess what the First Order wants? That's right, **control of the galaxy.**

One of the leaders of the First Order is **KYLO REN.** Even if you don't know much about him, you probably know all about his grandfather— **Darth Vader.** Kylo Ren wants to be **just as evil** as Vader was.

Luckily Princess Leia is still around, but she goes by **General Organa** these days, and she's the leader of a **new group** of rebellious heroes. They are known as …

the Resistance!

Now meet the RESISTANCE

YOU WILL NOTICE SOME FAMILIAR FACES IN THE RESISTANCE, BUT THERE ARE SOME OTHERS YOU MAY NOT KNOW SO WELL!

GENERAL ORGANA
Leia Organa **founded** the Resistance. She uses her experience as a rebel to be a **great leader.**

VICE ADMIRAL HOLDO
Amilyn Holdo is a shrewd **strategist.** She is loyal to her cause and **not** easily INTIMIDATED.

LIEUTENANT CONNIX

Kaydel Connix is a **hard-working** member of the Resistance. She always knows what's going on.

POE DAMERON

Poe is one of the star pilots of the Resistance, and he has the **confidence** to match his starfighter skills.

FINN

Stormtrooper-turned-hero, Finn is proud to fight **against** his former employers in the First Order.

REY

Scavenger Rey has street-smarts, a deadly quarterstaff, and unexpected **Force powers.**

RUNNING the Resistance is *not easy.* By their very nature, rebels **do not like** being told what to do. And when a **new leader** comes to town, **tensions** can run HIGH.

Everyone might have the Resistance's **best interests** at heart, but people have *very different* ways of doing things.

Some rebel leaders like to keep their plans **closely guarded,** while other rebels like to know what **everyone** is up to. Poe, for example, likes to know exactly what's going on at all times. He has a hard time accepting leaders won't always tell him everything. **Calm down, Poe!**

Hey!

SECRET PLANS

Communication is key: **trust** your **teammates,** give clear instructions, and ask for feedback. Whatever you do, don't start a rebellion within a rebellion. It's too confusing!

*I need to be charged.

Small, **upstart** rebel movements like the Resistance always welcome new recruits … **wherever** they come from.

Finn was a stormtrooper, but but he *didn't like* being mean to others or attacking innocent people, so he defected. After being a **fake** Resistance member for a while, Finn joined the crew **FOR REAL,** bringing along Rey and her mighty Force powers.

Rey was brought up on **stories** of the **Rebel Alliance,** so she can't believe she actually gets to be part of the Resistance!

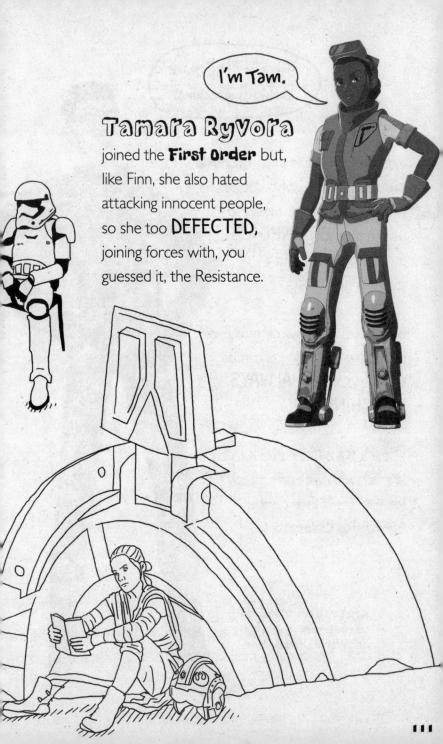

I'm Tam.

Tamara Ryvora

joined the **First Order** but, like Finn, she also hated attacking innocent people, so she too **DEFECTED**, joining forces with, you guessed it, the Resistance.

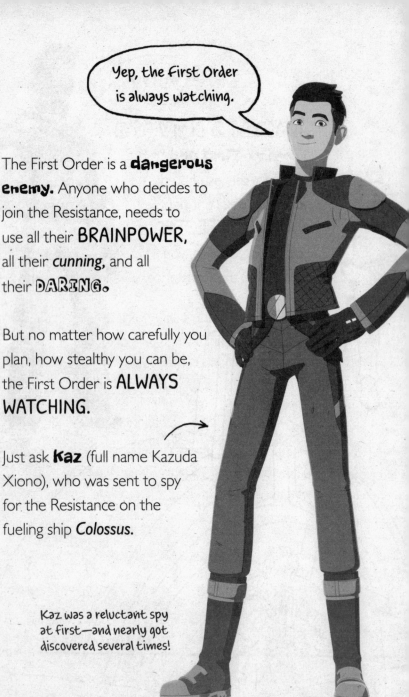

Yep, the First Order is always watching.

The First Order is a **dangerous enemy.** Anyone who decides to join the Resistance, needs to use all their **BRAINPOWER,** all their *cunning,* and all their **DARING.**

But no matter how carefully you plan, how stealthy you can be, the First Order is **ALWAYS WATCHING.**

Just ask **Kaz** (full name Kazuda Xiono), who was sent to spy for the Resistance on the fueling ship *Colossus.*

Kaz was a reluctant spy at first—and nearly got discovered several times!

Finn and Rose know all about the First Order. They know it isn't easy going **undercover** right under *Captain Phasma's* shiny silver nose, into the heart of the First Order flagship, working with an **unknown computer hacker** who's told you to just call him DJ. But hey, someone's gotta do it …

DJ

Suits you.

Really? I'm not sure about the hat.

Rose and Finn disguise themselves as First Order officers. Very stealthy!

Welcome to
THE
BATTLE OF *Crait*

FIRST ORDER WALKERS!

SPEEDERS!

Salty!

A <u>VERY</u> BIG GUN!

A SECRET BASE!

Attacking the mighty **First Order** is no easy task, but the Resistance has built **a network** of *really useful allies,* who help out where they can.

RECOGNIZE THESE GUYS?

Han and Chewie have gone back to their **smuggling ways.** But when the **NEW THREAT** of the First Order rises, you couldn't keep them away.

Argghghgg!*

I'm back! OK...
I'll help defeat the
bad guys again...

* Yippee!

Maz Kanata is an old friend of Han's (and I mean really old—she just celebrated her 1,001st birthday, weren't you invited?). She runs an **underworld hangout,** which means she knows just about everything that's going on. EVERYWHERE. WITH EVERYONE.

How can I help?

Old buddy, old pal, I'm back on the team!

Oh, and don't forget **Lando Calrissian.** He answers the call and joins the Resistance, too, **cape and all.**

Being part of the Resistance can be **tough** and **scary** (especially when you catch a glimpse of First Order Supreme Leader Snoke's face).

Boo!

But it's also **exciting** and **rewarding** to take part in even the smallest battle against the First Order.

If there's anything a member of the Resistance needs to know, it's this: **BE PREPARED. FOR ANYTHING.**

Like a giant **vexis serpent**, for example? Yup. Like realizing how cute **porgs** are? Yep.

Like ...

{SPOILER ALERT!}

... discovering **Emperor Palpatine** is **not actually dead?** Wait—whaaaat?

As part of the Resistance you need to get over your shock in mere seconds, and more importantly, **be prepared to take action!** Before the action takes you ...

And remember, it doesn't matter whether you **WIN** or **LOSE,** it's how you play the game.

OK, actually, I guess it **DOES** matter *a little bit* whether you win or lose, right? I mean, it is the **fate of the galaxy** we're talking about here.

So keep your eye on the prize and **never give up.**
Above all else, know that your rebellion against evil might
inspire people from the dustiest, windiest, frostiest,
swampiest parts of the galaxy to see what you've achieved
and maybe … just maybe … join the cause.

The end.
For now …

Glossary

ALLIANCE
A relationship or organization formed between different groups to achieve a shared goal.

ARCHIVE
Location for storing old documents or historical records.

ASTROMECH DROID
A type of robot designed to help repair and navigate starfighters.

BATTALION
A unit of soldiers, usually no more than 1,000.

BOUNTY HUNTER
People who look for, capture, and sometimes destroy, other people for a reward—usually money.

Watch out!

CADET
A young trainee, or pupil, often in the military or police services.

CIVIL WAR
A war between different people, usually in one country. The Galactic Civil War divided the whole galaxy as the Rebel Alliance sought to bring an end to the Empire and restore freedom to all.

CLONE WARS
A war between the Republic and its enemies that ended with the Republic becoming the Empire.

COMPACTOR
Something that makes garbage smaller by squashing it.

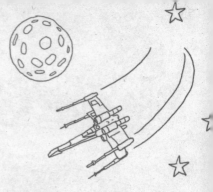

DEFECT
Leave or abandon a group or organization, often joining a rival group, after a change in beliefs.

DEMOCRACY
A system of government that is fair and just, where people get to choose their leaders, usually via elections.

DICTATORSHIP
A type of leadership, or government, where the decisions are all made by one leader or small group of leaders.

EMPEROR
Ruler of the Empire.

EMPIRE
A tyrannical power that rules the galaxy under the leadership of Emperor Palpatine, a Sith Lord.

ENLIST
To request someone's help for something.

EXPENDABLE
Considered not important, and as such can be abandoned or disposed of once used.

FLEET
A group of vehicles, such as sailing ships or starships, owned by the same group of people.

FORCE
A mysterious energy that exists in all living things; can be used by the Jedi and the Sith.

HOLOGRAM
A projected 3D image of a person or object that is not there physically.

Boo! Down with the Empire!

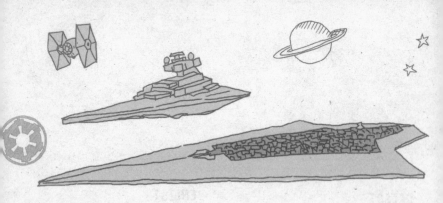

HYPERSPACE
A method that ships use to travel faster than the speed of light.

JEDI
A being who studies the light side of the Force and uses their powers for good.

KESSEL RUN
A dangerous route through space, famously completed very quickly by Han Solo.

IMPERIAL
Relating to the Empire.

Shhh!

INFILTRATE
Enter a place secretly.

LIGHTSABER
A swordlike weapon with a blade of pure energy, used by both Jedi and Sith.

MIND TRICK
A way a Force-user can make weak-minded people obey them.

PERSONNEL
People employed to look after other people, often in the military.

I'm the Kessel Run champ!

PROTOCOL DROID
A robot designed to help with communications.

REPUBLIC
The former, fair, democratic government that ruled most planets in the galaxy.

SCAVENGER
Someone who collects junk.

SITH
A being who uses the dark side of the Force for evil purposes.

SMUGGLER
Someone who takes goods to or from a place illegally and sells them for profit.

TRANSMIT
Broadcast or send out a message, such as via radio signal.

TYRANNY
An unfair, cruel rule from people in power, sometimes a government.

UNDERWORLD
The world of criminals.

Here is my plan for a NEW, upgraded Death Star!
The rebels will never see this coming ...